JP Taylo

Taylor, J.
Penguin's special Christmas
tree.

Penguin's Special Christmas Tree

written by

Jeannie St. John Taylor

illustrated by Molly Idle

Lobster Press™

Published by Lobster Press™
1620 Sherbrooke Street West, Suites C & D
Montréal, Québec   H3H 1C9
Tel. (514) 904-1100 • Fax (514) 904-1101
www.lobsterpress.com

Publisher: Alison Fripp
Editors: Alison Fripp & Meghan Nolan
Editorial Assistant: Faye Smailes
Graphic Design & Production: Tammy Desnoyers

Société
de développement
des entreprises
culturelles
Québec

We acknowledge the support of the government of Québec, tax credit for book publishing, administered by SODEC.

Library and Archives Canada Cataloguing in Publication

St. John Taylor, Jeannie, 1945-
    Penguin's special Christmas tree / Jeannie St. John Taylor ; Molly Idle, illustrator.

ISBN 978-1-897073-61-2 (bound)
ISBN 978-1-897073-64-3 (pbk.)

    1. Penguins--Juvenile fiction. 2. Christmas stories, American. I. Idle, Molly Schaar II. Title.

PZ7.T357Pe 2007   j813'.6   C2007-901251-5

Printed and bound in Singapore.

To Ty, Tori, Tevin, and Kirsten

– *Jeannie St. John Taylor*

For Evan and Randy

– *Molly Idle*

"I want to **win** 'Santa's Best Tree' award this year, but I can't find anything for the **top** of the tree."

"I'll think of something ...

I'm thinking ...

Still thinking ...

Got it!"

"Santa *loves* handmade stuff."

"Not enough color?"

"This just won't work.
Let's try a smaller snowman."

"*This* size is better."

"I'll get the mop."

"Nobody else will have something like this on the top!"

"Wait!"

"I know!
Let's put Harold on top!"

"Great idea!"

"Harold *monkeys* around too much."

"Maybe we need something
that lights up!"

"Wait until you see **this!**"

"Are you out of ideas now?"

"Yes."

"Me too. I'll never finish in time. I'm so sad! I *really* want to **win** the **award**! What will I do?"

"I wish I knew how to help."

"Hey! Wait. GREAT idea.
Stay there. Don't move.
Up a little higher.
Move that way.
A little more ... more.
Too much. Go back.

Perfect!"

"Yes!"

"You won!
Santa loves your tree!"

"We won.
I couldn't have done it without you."